Wee Willie
Winkie III

written by Nancy Wiedmeyer

llustrations by Trudy Perry

MINDSTIR MEDIA

Wee Willie Winkie III
Copyright © 2018 Nancy Wiedmeyer. All rights reserved.

llustrations by Trudy Perry

Published by Mindstir Media, LLC
45 Lafayette Rd | Suite 181| North Hampton, NH 03862 | USA
1.800.767.0531 | www.mindstirmedia.com

Printed in the United States of America
ISBN-13: 978-0-9996085-6-2
Library of Congress Control Number: 2017918850

Dedicated to all my furry and feathered friends

Wee Willie Winkie is a Scottish nursery rhyme. The poem was written by William Miller and titled, "Willie Winkie" in 1841. The original text below is different from the English version that appeared in 1844.

Wee Willie Winkie rins through the toon,
Upstairs an' doon stairs in his nicht-gown,
Tirlin' at the window, crying at the lock,
"Are the weans in their bed, for it's noo ten o'clock?"

"Hey, Willie Winkie, are ye comin' ben?
The cat's singin grey thrums to the sleepin hen,
The dog's speldert on the floor and disna gie a cheep,
But here's a waukrife laddie, that wunna fa' asleep."

Wee Willie Winkie became very popular as a bedtime poem. Tirlin' at the window refers to a form of door bell. It was scraped up and down on the door to make a rattling sound to announce a visitor.

This is the English version from the book of Mother Goose.

Wee Willie Winkie runs through the town,
Upstairs and downstairs, in his nightgown;
Tapping at the window, crying at the lock;
"Are the babes in their beds, for it's now ten o'clock?".

Hey, Willie Winkie, are you coming in?
The cat is singing purring sounds to the sleeping hen,
The dog's spread out on the floor, and doesn't give a cheep,
But here's a wakeful little boy who will not fall asleep!

This is the story of Wee Willie Winkie III.
Willie was my Basset Hound and his registered
name was Wee Willie Winkie V.

Yes, I am the real Wee Willie Winkie! Actually, I'm Wee Willie Winkie III. I come from a long line of Wee Willie Winkies. But everyone calls me just plain Willie.

I run through the town quite often. Sometimes six or seven times a day. Being a young Basset Hound, I like to check things out and play with my friends.

I tried playing with a silly skunk named Stinky, but he just turned away from me and lifted his tail.

Ozzie, a burly little brown mixed breed, lives two houses down the street from me. JC, a white terrier, lives across the street from Ozzie. We three have a grand time running in the park and chasing each other.

Once in a while, Bugs, a brown rabbit from the forest, gets into the fun.

I do run upstairs and downstairs following Benny, my human friend, but I don't wear a nightgown. That's ridiculous! Dogs don't wear nightgowns. I have very nice black and white fur that fits me perfectly. I have no idea how that rumor started.

It may sound like I'm rapping at the window or door when my tail wags and hits them. I have quite a strong tail and it does wag a lot. I can use my paws and toenails to scrape the window.

I'm not crying at the locks of the doors, simply making noise so Benny will hear me and let me inside. I howl pretty well, especially when the town siren blows at noon. My friends, Ozzie and JC join me and I must say, we sound pretty awesome.

∞

Around ten o'clock, I am tired from my busy day. It has gone by so quickly. Benny asks me, "Are you coming in?"

The cat, Whiskers, is already purring and sleeping on the brown chair, tired of running after Molly, our little hen.

I am spread out on the rug on the floor when Benny calls me to his bed. He is not tired but I snuggle with him.

Good night.
Sweet dreams.

Printed in the USA
CPSIA information can be obtained
at www.ICGtesting.com
LVHW071932191023
761583LV00018B/300